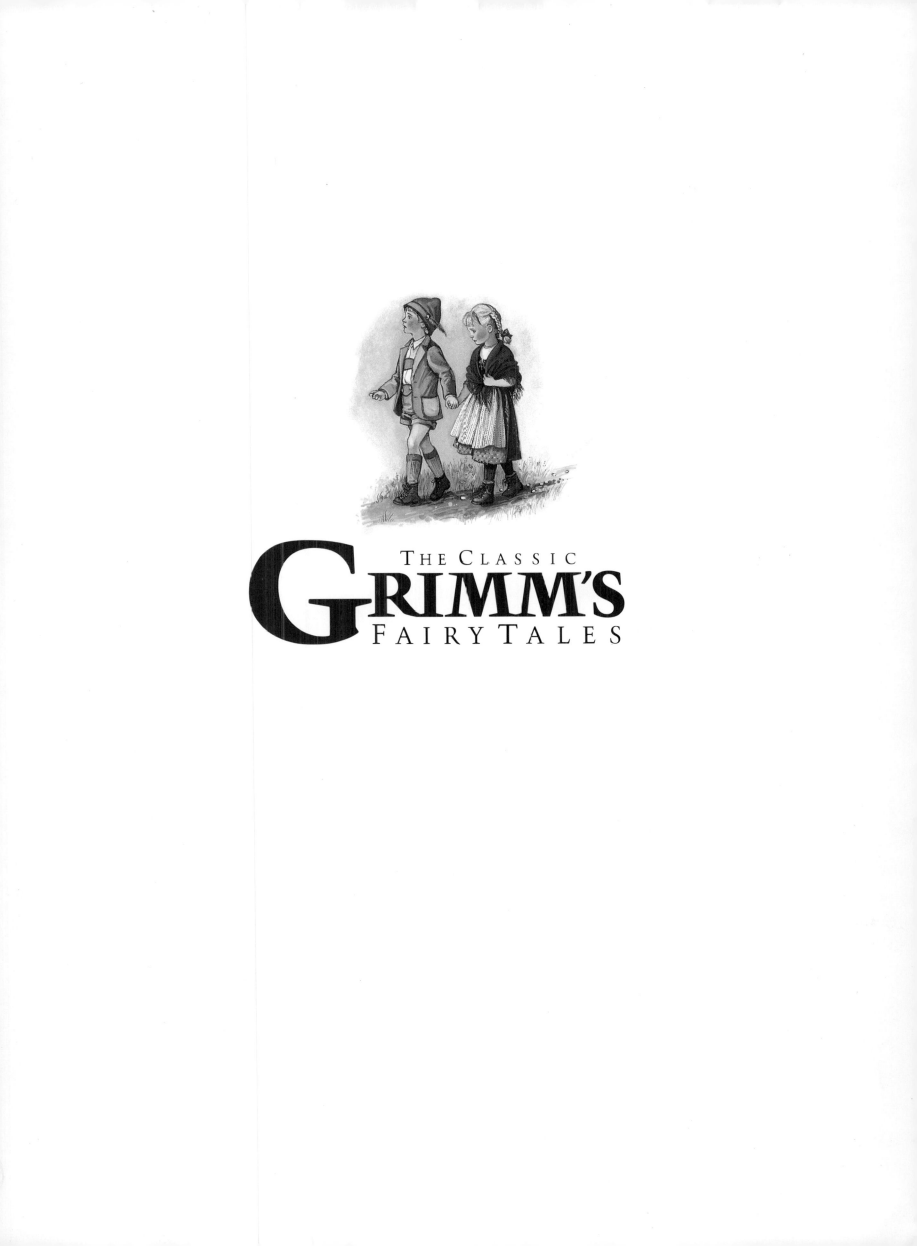

THE CLASSIC
GRIMM'S
FAIRY TALES

THE CLASSIC
GRIMM'S
FAIRY TALES

Retold by Louise Betts Egan

Illustrated by
ERIN WISE

KAREN PRITCHETT

KAY LIFE

JADA ROWLAND

ARLENE KLEMUSHIN

JULIA NOONAN

RICHARD WALZ

Produced By Ariel Books

COURAGE
BOOKS
AN IMPRINT OF RUNNING PRESS
PHILADELPHIA • LONDON

Retold by Louise Betts Egan

Canadian representatives: General Publishing Co., Ltd., 30 Lesmill Road,
Don Mills, Ontario M3B 2T6.

20 19 18 17 16 15 14 13 12

Digit on the right indicates the number of this printing.

Library of Congress Cataloging-in-Publication Number
89–43005

ISBN 0–89471–768–5 (Cloth)

Printed in Hong Kong
Jacket and interior designed by Michael Hortens
Art direction by Armand Eisen
Jacket illustration by Robyn Officer

Published by Courage Books, an imprint of Running Press
Book Publishers, 125 South Twenty-second Street, Philadelphia, PA 19103.

FOREWORD

The stories in this book are called "Grimm's Fairy Tales." They are named after Jacob and Wilhelm Grimm, two brothers from Germany who lived over two hundred years ago. Their stories are about strange and fanciful things that happened "once upon a time."

The Grimm brothers collected these tales from friends and strangers, old and young, rich and poor. In their day, stories were mostly passed on from memory. The Grimms were the first to write the stories down, and parents have been reading these tales to their children ever since.

In Grimm's tales there are giants and elves, witches and fairies, talking animals, and enchanted fish. But it is the people—like Snow White, Hansel and Gretel, and Little Red Riding Hood—that we remember best. We like these characters and don't want them hurt by evil stepmothers, witches, or wolves. How they escape their troubles is important to us. We learn from them.

So, settle back against your pillow and pull your blanket around you. It is storytime now, and time to enter the magical world of the Brothers Grimm.

LOUISE BETTS EGAN

CONTENTS

The Classic

CINDERELLA

A wealthy widower married for the second time. The man's new wife was haughty, cruel, and selfish, as were her two ugly daughters. All three women deeply disliked the man's only daughter, a lovely girl who had all of her mother's goodness.

The stepmother immediately began to make the girl's once happy life a hard and miserable one. First, she took away the girl's fine clothes, giving her instead an old gray smock and wooden shoes to wear. The girl was then forced to work from morning 'til night, washing, cleaning, and cooking, as well as carrying out whatever whims her stepmother and stepsisters asked.

Because she was forced to sleep on the stone hearth next to the ashes and cinders, her mother and stepsisters gave her the name Cinderella.

One day, the king announced that he was giving a ball. In the hope that his son might find a suitable bride, all the noble ladies of the kingdom were invited. For weeks, the cruel stepsisters kept Cinderella busy with their preparations and taunted her endlessly because she would not be going.

On the night of the ball, they called Cinderella. "Comb our hair, brush our shoes, and fasten our gowns!" they said. "We're going to meet the prince!"

Cinderella did as she was told. But she could not help wishing with all her heart that she too were going to the ball. When the stepmother and her daughters had gone, the girl sank down on the cold stone hearth and wept.

At that moment, a soft light filled the room. Cinderella looked up and beheld a beautiful being dressed in a shimmering robe and holding a sparkling wand.

"I'm your fairy godmother," the magical being said. "Are you crying because you want to go to the ball?" Cinderella nodded.

"Then you shall cry no more," the fairy godmother said.

She asked Cinderella to bring her a pumpkin from the garden. When Cinderella brought back the finest pumpkin on the vine, the godmother touched it with the tip of her wand and it turned into a magnificent, gilded coach.

Before Cinderella's astonished eyes, six mice were turned into a team of fine horses; a rat became a distinguished coachman; and four garden lizards were turned into elegant footmen, all with a single touch of the magic wand.

Cinderella than glanced down at her dirty, ragged clothes. Before she could say a word, the fairy godmother's wand changed Cinderella into a dazzling princess, with a gown frosted with jewels. On the young girl's tiny feet were a pair of exquisite glass slippers.

"Oh, Fairy Godmother, however can I thank you?" Cinderella exclaimed.

The fairy godmother just smiled and said, "Enjoy the ball, but you must come home by the last stroke of midnight! If you don't, your coach will once more be a pumpkin and your beautiful gown will turn to rags."

Cinderella promised to return by midnight, and off she sped in the coach to the king's palace.

By the time Cinderella arrived at the ball, the prince had grown bored and restless. He had not met one young lady who had interested him in the least. But as soon as Cinderella entered the room, his eyes lit up.

The prince was not the only one to notice the newcomer; when she stood at the door in her sparkling gown, all heads turned and a hush fell over the room. Everyone wanted to know who the beautiful princess was.

Though Cinderella could not tell the prince her name or where she came from, he was enchanted by her all the same. They danced as long as the music played, and talked of many things.

For the rest of the evening, the prince kept Cinderella by his side. Everyone wondered who she could be, but even her stepsisters did not recognize her.

Cinderella was enjoying herself so much that she forgot all about the time. But when the bell on the clock tower began to strike twelve, Cinderella jumped. She made a quick curtsey to the prince and dashed out of the ballroom.

"Please, stop!" called the prince. But Cinderella ran away as fast as she could.

On the castle steps, Cinderella glanced down and saw that her gown was beginning to turn back to rags. She stumbled, leaving behind one of her glass slippers. After the coach had turned back into a pumpkin, Cinderella walked the rest of the way home.

The prince was determined to find the enchanting princess whom he had met at the ball. For weeks afterwards, he searched the kingdom for the woman whose dainty foot fit the glass slipper left on the castle steps.

One day, he came to Cinderella's house. The cruel stepsisters tried to squeeze their large feet into the slipper, but to no avail. Then, just as he was about to leave, the prince noticed a girl in ragged clothing and bare feet.

"That's only Cinderella," said the stepmother. "Never mind her!" But the prince asked her to come forward.

Cinderella slid her foot into the slipper, and it fit perfectly. It was then that the prince saw, through her dirt and rags, the beautiful princess he had met at the ball. He asked her to marry him and she happily accepted.

The cruel stepmother and her daughters immediately fell to their knees to ask Cinderella's forgiveness. But the prince just laughed at them. He ordered his servants to drive them out of the kingdom, and they were never seen again.

LITTLE RED RIDING HOOD

—⚬⚭—

There was once a sweet little girl who was loved by everyone. As a present, the girl's grandmother made her a little riding hood of red velvet. The cap pleased the girl so much that she always wore it and so she became known as Little Red Riding Hood.

One day, her mother asked her to take a basket of cakes and wine to her grandmother. "She has been sick and weak," her mother said, "and this food will surely strengthen her."

But before Little Red Riding Hood set out, her mother warned her to be good and not to stray from the path. "You may get lost or trip and fall, and then your grandmother will get nothing."

Little Red Riding Hood promised to obey her mother's wishes, and off she went, skipping through the forest. She had not gone far when she came upon a wolf. Not knowing what a wicked animal he was, she gave him a friendly greeting and told him she was going to visit her grandmother on the other side of the woods.

When the wolf heard this, he was pleased, for he was very hungry and now he could look forward to two delicious meals: Little Red Riding Hood and her grandmother. But he was a clever wolf, and was careful not to alarm the child.

Instead, the wolf walked along beside her and spoke in a soft voice. "Isn't the forest lovely today?" he said. "Look at all the beautiful flowers! It would be a pity to hurry past them."

Little Red Riding Hood looked around and saw how right the wolf was. Sunbeams danced through the trees, the birds were singing merrily, and there were flowers everywhere.

"Grandmother would certainly like a nice bunch of wildflowers," Little Red Riding Hood thought to herself. And so she skipped off the path and began gathering a big bouquet.

Meanwhile, the wolf sped through the woods all the way to the grandmother's cottage and knocked on the door.

"Who's there?" cried the grandmother in her weak voice.

"It is I, Little Red Riding Hood!" cried the wolf.

So the grandmother opened the door, and the wolf swallowed her in a single gulp. Then he put on her nightgown and her lace cap, and settled down to wait for Little Red Riding Hood.

When Little Red Riding Hood reached her grandmother's cottage, she was surprised to find the door wide open. She poked her head in and looked around.

"Good morning, Grandmother!" she called. But there was no answer. Feeling a little frightened, Little Red Riding Hood went to her grandmother's room.

"Oh, Grandmother, what big ears you have!" she cried.

"The better to hear you with," said the wolf.

"But, Grandmother, what big eyes you have!"

"All the better to see you with," said the wolf.

"But, Grandmother! What big teeth you have!"

"The better to eat you with!"

With that, the wolf sprang out of bed and gobbled up poor Little Red Riding Hood in a single swallow. After that, the wolf was so full that he lay back down on the bed and fell into a heavy sleep.

Now, it happened that a huntsman was passing by and, seeing the cottage door open, he became suspicious. Carefully, he went inside, and there he found the wolf lying asleep in the grandmother's bed.

He was about to shoot the wolf dead with his rifle, when he suddenly thought the wolf might have eaten the grandmother, and that perhaps she could still be saved. So he took out his knife and carefully cut open the wolf's belly.

Out jumped Little Red Riding Hood. "Thank you!" she exclaimed. "It was so dark inside the wolf!"

Out came the grandmother as well, who was still alive, although she was feeling rather weak.

Little Red Riding Hood quickly fetched some large stones. These she placed inside the sleeping wolf's belly, and the hunter sewed him up again. When the wolf awoke and tried to run away, he was so heavy that he fell down at once and died. The hunter, Little Red Riding Hood, and her grandmother all danced for joy.

Then the brave huntsman skinned the wolf and took the fur home. The grandmother ate the cakes and drank the wine, which made her feel much stronger. As for Little Red Riding Hood, she skipped happily all the way home. But she had learned her lesson, for she never strayed from the path again!

RUMPELSTILTSKIN

There was once a poor miller whose daughter was so beautiful, the king himself came to see her. The miller, hoping the king might wish to make the daughter his bride, bragged to him: "Not only is my daughter lovely—she can spin straw into gold!"

When the king heard this, he ordered that the girl be brought to his castle.

When the miller's daughter arrived at the castle, the king showed her to a room filled to the ceiling with straw. In the corner was a spinning wheel. "Now get to work!" he said. "But I warn you, if you don't spin this straw into gold by morning, you shall lose your life." Then he locked the door and left the girl inside all alone.

The poor girl began to weep, for she knew nothing about turning straw into gold. Suddenly, the door opened and a dwarf entered the room.

"Why are you crying?" he asked. When the girl told him, the dwarf said, "What will you give me if I spin it for you?"

The girl promised him the necklace around her neck, and so the dwarf set to work, whir, whir, whir! By morning, the straw was spun into gold and the dwarf had vanished.

The king was surprised and delighted. But the sight of so much gold made him even greedier. He led the girl to a still larger room filled with straw and said: "If you value your life, you will

spin all this straw into gold by morning."

No sooner had the king left the room when the dwarf appeared again. This time, the girl gave him the ring from her finger. Once more, the little man spinned all through the night, and disappeared the moment the job was done.

When the king entered the room the next morning, he had to shield his eyes from the brilliance of all the gold about him. He was very impressed, but still he hungered for more.

He led the miller's daughter to an even bigger room filled with straw and once again ordered her to spin it into gold by morning. "If you succeed," he told her, "I will make you my wife." For even though she was just a common girl, he was sure he would never find a richer bride.

When the young girl was alone, the dwarf appeared once more.

"But I have nothing more to give you," said the poor girl.

"Just promise me your firstborn child," replied the dwarf.

The girl did so, for she doubted that such a thing would ever come to pass. So the little man spinned all the straw into gold. The king then married her, and the miller's beautiful daughter became a queen.

A year passed, and the queen forgot the funny little man who had helped her. But when she had her first child, the dwarf appeared before her and demanded that she keep her promise.

The queen pleaded with him. "I will give you anything," she said, "all the treasures in the world, but please, let me keep my child!"

The little man just shook his head and replied, "A living thing is worth more to me than all the treasure in the world."

This made the queen weep so bitterly that at last the dwarf felt sorry for her.

"Very well," said he. "I will give you three days in which to guess my name, and if you do, you may keep your child."

On the first day, the queen guessed every name she ever knew. But to all of them, the little man replied, "That's not my name."

On the second day, the queen sent all her servants into the kingdom to find as many names as they could, and some of the names were very strange indeed.

"Is your name Ribsofbeef or Muttonchops?" she asked the dwarf.

But to each he only replied, "That's not my name."

On the eve of the third day, the queen was beside herself with grief. She could think of no more names, and did not know what to do.

Then, at dawn, a messenger came to the queen with a strange story. The night before, as he rode through the forest, he had seen a funny little man dancing around a fire. As he danced, the little man had sung:

"Today I'll brew, tomorrow I'll bake.
Soon I'll have the queen's namesake.
Oh, how hard it is to play my game,
for Rumpelstiltskin is my name!"

When she heard this, the queen was overjoyed. That day, when the dwarf appeared, ready to take the child, she said: "Is your name Henry?"

"That's not my name," said the dwarf with a smile.

"Very well then, is it Karl?"

"That's not my name."

"Then can it be . . . Rumpelstiltskin?"

When he heard this, the dwarf screamed with rage. "The devil must have told you!" And then he stamped his foot so hard that he broke right in two. And that was the end of Rumpelstiltskin.

SNOW WHITE

One winter's day long, long ago, a queen sat sewing by a castle window. It was snowing outside, and she liked looking up and seeing the white, feathery snowflakes gather on the shiny ebony window frame. Suddenly, she pricked herself with her needle. She opened the window to cool her sore finger, and three drops of blood fell onto the snow.

The queen smiled and thought, "If only I had a child with skin as white as snow, cheeks as red as blood, and hair as black as ebony!"

In time, a daughter was born who looked just as the queen had wished. The queen named her little girl Snow White. Unfortunately, the queen died soon after the child was born.

Within a year, the king remarried. His new queen was very beautiful but she was also cruel and proud. This wicked queen had a magic mirror and she would often look into it and ask:

"Mirror, mirror on the wall,
who is the fairest one of all?"

Then the mirror would answer:

"You, my queen, are the fairest of all."

This reply always satisfied the queen, for she knew the mirror never lied.

The years went by and Snow White grew lovelier each day. The wicked queen was jealous of Snow White, but never more so than when the queen asked her mirror one day who was the fairest in the land.

The mirror replied:

"You, my queen, may have a beauty quite rare,
but Snow White is a thousand times more fair."

The queen was filled with rage and envy. From that moment on she knew no peace, for her hatred of Snow White grew stronger every day. At last, the queen called one of her huntsmen to her. She told him to take Snow White deep into the forest and kill her with his knife. "To prove that she is dead," she told him, "you must bring me her heart."

The huntsman led Snow White deep into the forest, but he could not bring himself to kill the beautiful girl. He simply left her there and warned her never to return home. Then he shot a deer and took its heart back to the queen, who threw it into the fire.

Meanwhile, Snow White wandered deeper and deeper into the woods. Dead tree branches stuck out like bony, crooked fingers. Wild animals scooted past her, grunting and growling. The poor girl was terribly frightened. She ran and ran, until she came upon a little cottage. When no one answered the door, she tiptoed inside.

The little house was lovely! Everything was dainty and neat and very small. There was a table set with a clean, white tablecloth, seven small plates, and seven little goblets. Over by the wall were seven little beds with fluffy covers.

Snow White was hungry, but even so, she only took a bite of food from each plate and a sip of wine from each goblet. She then went over to the beds and tried each one, until she found one that was comfortable. Soon Snow White was fast asleep.

A short while later seven little dwarfs came marching and singing into the cottage. They were most startled to see Snow White asleep on the bed, but the little men were so taken with her beauty that they did not wake her.

The next morning, Snow White was afraid when she saw the seven dwarfs around her. But they were so kindhearted that she soon told them her sad story. The seven dwarfs then invited her to live with them, provided she do the cooking and housework. Snow White gratefully agreed.

Each morning, the dwarfs left the house early and went to the mountains, where they mined for minerals and gold. They warned Snow White never to let anyone into the cottage.

"Your wicked stepmother will soon discover you're here, beware!" they told her.

Back at the castle, the queen picked up her mirror and asked who was the fairest of all. To her surprise, The mirror replied:

"You, my queen, may have a beauty quite rare,
but beyond the mountains, where the seven dwarfs dwell,
Snow White is thriving, and this I must tell:
Within this land, she's still a thousand times more fair."

The queen instantly realized that the huntsman had deceived her. Trembling with fury, she vowed to kill Snow White and soon came up with a plan.

She dressed herself up as a poor peasant woman selling apples. Then she crossed the seven mountains to the seven dwarfs' cottage, where she knocked on the door and called out, "Apples! Lovely apples!"

Snow White looked out the window and said, "Please go away. I'm not allowed to let anyone in!"

"Never mind," said the peasant woman. "I'll leave you this apple as a gift."

Snow White started to refuse, but the apple looked so rosy and beautiful that she hesitated. "Here," said the wicked queen, "let me show you how good the apple is." She picked it up, cut it in half, and took a bite. The apple had been so cunningly made that her half was harmless, while the other half contained poison.

When Snow White saw the woman eat the apple, she accepted the other half. But no sooner did the girl take a bite of it than she fell down dead.

The queen quickly returned home and asked her mirror, *"Now* who is the fairest in the land?" The mirror replied, "You, my queen, are the fairest of all."

The dwarfs were heartbroken to find their dear Snow White dead, and they wept for three days. They intended to bury her, but Snow White looked so alive, and her cheeks were still so red, that they put her in a glass coffin and carried it to the top of a woodland mound.

For many years, Snow White lay in the coffin. She still looked as lovely as ever, as though she were not dead, but only sleeping.

One day, a prince came to the forest. When he saw Snow White in the coffin, he begged the dwarfs to let him take her back to his castle. He pleaded so desperately that at last the dwarfs agreed.

The prince and his servants carried Snow White along the forest paths in her coffin. Suddenly, one of the servants tripped and the coffin fell to the ground. The piece of poison apple was jolted from Snow White's throat, and she sat up and looked around in amazement. The prince and the dwarfs were overjoyed.

The prince knelt at Snow White's side and told her how much he loved her. When he asked her to be his wife, Snow White happily agreed and put her hands in his.

That day, the wicked queen gazed proudly into her mirror and asked who was the fairest of all.

The mirror replied:

"Fairest is she who, though she died,
now lives to be the prince's bride."

The queen was so furious that she hurled the mirror to the ground. And her cruel heart shattered into a thousand pieces.

THE BREMEN TOWN MUSICIANS

Once upon a time there was a donkey whose master had made him carry heavy sacks to the mill for many years. One day, he overheard his master say that as the donkey was now old and could no longer do the work, he planned to get rid of him as soon as he could.

But the donkey did not wait around to reap such a dreadful reward. Instead, he set off for Bremen, where he thought he could perform as a town musician. On the way, he came upon a poor old hound lying by the side of the road. The hound was panting as if he had just run a long way.

"Why are you so out of breath?" asked the donkey.

"Oh, dear!" cried the dog. "I have just escaped from my master. He was going to have me killed because I am old and can no longer hunt. But whatever will I do now?"

"Come with me!" said the donkey. "I'm going to Bremen to become a town musician, and I could use another voice."

The dog happily agreed and off they went. Before long, they came upon a sad gray cat sitting in the road.

The cat sighed and said, "I'm no use any more. My teeth are blunt, and I would rather sit by the hearth and purr than catch mice. My mistress wanted to drown me! So I've left home but now I have nowhere to go."

"Come with us to Bremen," said the donkey. "We're musicians and I'm sure you know how to sing a fine song!"

The cat agreed, and the three animals continued on their way.

As they passed a farmyard, they heard a rooster crowing with all his might.

"Your crows are enough to pierce a bone!" exclaimed the donkey.

"I have only a few hours left to crow at all," said the rooster sadly. "My mistress told the cook that tomorrow I must be made into soup!"

The rooster was immediately invited to come with them to Bremen, and he happily accepted.

But Bremen was too far off to be reached in one day. And so toward evening, they began to look for a place to spend the night. At last, they settled on a large tree in the woods. The donkey and the dog lay at its foot, the cat climbed up among the branches, and the rooster flew right to the top.

But before the rooster went to sleep, he looked east, west, north, and south, as was his habit. Suddenly, he spied a light shining from a house in the distance, and he called down to his friends.

The animals, eager for a more comfortable spot to pass the night, quicky agreed to head toward the house. But when they arrived and peered through the windows, they realized that it was not an ordinary house, but a robbers' den! Inside, there was nothing but a fireplace and a long table. Around the table sat the robbers, feasting on all kinds of delicacies and counting out the money they had stolen.

"I think this house will suit us fine," said the rooster.

The others agreed, and so they devised a plan to frighten away the robbers. The donkey placed his forefeet on the windowsill, and the dog climbed on his back. The cat stood on top of the dog, and the rooster flew up and perched on the cat's head. Then all of them began to sing

33

as loud as they could. The donkey brayed, the dog barked, the cat meowed, and the rooster crowed. Their music made such a noise that the robbers were sure a ghost or goblin had come to haunt the place. Terrified, they ran away as fast as they could.

The four companions then went into the house and gobbled up the remains of the robbers' feast. Their bellies full, they all lay down for the night. The donkey settled outside by the stable. The dog stretched out behind the door. The cat settled beside the warm hearth, and the rooster perched on the roof.

Soon, they were all fast asleep.

Meanwhile, the robbers were watching the house from the woods. As the hours passed, their leader began to feel silly for having been so frightened. When he saw that no light was burning and that all was quiet, he sent one of his men to explore the house.

Quietly, the robber crept into the kitchen to light a candle. But he mistook the cat's glowing, fiery eyes for live coals. When he held a match to them, however, the cat leaped into the robber's face, spitting and scratching as fiercely as he could. The man was so terrified that he ran to the back door and straight into the dog. The startled hound gave him a hard bite on the leg. Howling with pain, the robber ran past the stable, where the donkey gave him a swift kick with his hind leg. All the noise woke up the rooster, who immediately crowed, "Cocka-doodle-doo!"

When the robber reached the others, he was trembling so hard that he could barely speak. "What happened?" they asked.

"There's a wicked witch in the house!" cried the poor man. "She spat on me and scratched my face with her long claws. At the door there's a man with a knife who stabbed me in the leg. Out in the yard is a big monster who beat me with a club. And the judge was sitting on top of the roof shouting, 'Bring that rascal here!'"

After that, none of the robbers dared return to the house ever again! But the four Bremen Town musicians liked the place so much that they decided to stay there forever, and, for all I know, they are there to this day.

RAPUNZEL

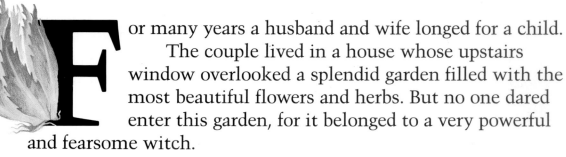

For many years a husband and wife longed for a child. The couple lived in a house whose upstairs window overlooked a splendid garden filled with the most beautiful flowers and herbs. But no one dared enter this garden, for it belonged to a very powerful and fearsome witch.

One day, as the wife stood at the window looking out over the garden, she spied some fine rapunzel lettuce. The rapunzel looked so fresh and green that her mouth tingled at the thought of eating some. Her craving for the rapunzel grew and grew. Knowing that she could never have any, the woman began to grow pale and weak.

Her husband, who feared she would die from the craving, decided he must get her some of the forbidden rapunzel. One night, he climbed down into the garden and stole a handful. His wife made it into a delicious salad, but this only made her crave the lettuce even more.

One night, at dusk the husband sneaked back into the garden and grabbed another handful of the delicious rapunzel. To his horror, he looked up and found the witch standing before him.

"How dare you climb into my garden and steal my rapunzel!" she cried angrily.

The husband begged for mercy and explained why he had stolen the lettuce.

"If that's true," said the witch, "you may take all the rapunzel you like, as long as you give me the child your wife will bear." In fear, the man agreed.

When the woman's baby was born, the witch appeared at once. She named the child Rapunzel and carried her away.

Rapunzel grew into a beautiful child with shimmering, golden hair. When she was twelve years old, the witch locked her up in a tall tower in the middle of the forest. The tower had neither door nor stairs, only one small window. Whenever the witch wanted to come up, she would stand at the foot of the tower and call out:

"Rapunzel, Rapunzel,
let down your long hair."

Rapunzel would then unbind her braids and drop her long, radiant hair out the window. When her hair touched the ground, the witch would climb up on it.

A few years later, a prince happened to be riding through the forest. Suddenly, he heard a song so lovely that he paused to listen. It was Rapunzel, whose sweet voice often echoed through the forest. The prince spotted her as she sang in the tower, but he could see no way of reaching her. At last, he rode away. However, the prince returned every day after that to hear Rapunzel sing.

One afternoon, the prince saw the witch go to the tower and call out:

"Rapunzel, Rapunzel,
let down your long hair."

He then watched as Rapunzel let her golden hair down and the witch climbed up to the window.

The next evening, when the witch had gone, the prince rode to the foot of the tower and called:

"Rapunzel, Rapunzel,
let down your long hair."

When the hair dropped down, the prince climbed up into the tower. At first, Rapunzel was frightened; she had never seen a man before. But the prince was so gentle and kind that her fears quickly vanished. In time, the prince asked Rapunzel to marry him, and she agreed.

Together, they devised a way for her to escape: On each visit, the prince would bring her a skein of silk, which she would weave into a ladder. When it was finished, she would climb down and ride off with the handsome prince.

The witch knew nothing of the prince and his courtship of Rapunzel. But one day the girl blurted out, "Why is it that the prince climbs up my hair so much faster than you?"

The witch was furious. "I thought I had hidden you from the world! You have betrayed me, you sinful child!" With that, the witch cut off Rapunzel's beautiful hair and whisked her away to a desolate land, where the girl lived in misery and despair.

On the same day on which she banished Rapunzel, the witch returned to the tower and tied the braids to a hook on the window. When the prince called that evening, she let down the long, golden hair. When the unsuspecting prince climbed up, it was not Rapunzel who met him, but the evil witch.

"Aha!" she exclaimed. "Your sweet bird no longer sits in her nest. The cat has her, and it will scratch your eyes out, too. You will see Rapunzel no more!"

Shocked and bewildered, the prince jumped from the tower window. He fell into some thorn bushes, which broke his fall and saved his life. But the long thorns on the bushes pierced his eyes and blinded him.

For years, the desperate prince roamed the forest, mourning the loss of his only love. One day, he wandered to the desert where the lonely Rapunzel was living.

Suddenly, the blind prince heard a familiar voice singing and went straight toward it. The voice was Rapunzel's. Seeing the prince, Rapunzel let out a cry of joy. She threw her arms around him and wept. When her tears touched his eyes, the prince could see again.

The prince took Rapunzel back to his kingdom, where they lived happily together.

THE SHOEMAKER AND THE ELVES

There was once a shoemaker who, through no fault of his own, had become so poor that he had only enough leather for one more pair of shoes.

"I will make these the best shoes I can!" he told himself. That night, he cut out the shoes and planned to sew them together in the morning. Then he kissed his wife good-night, blew out the candle, and crawled into bed. Being a kind and honest man, the shoemaker had no trouble sleeping soundly through the night.

He awoke the next morning, ready to begin work. But when he got to his workbench, he could hardly believe his eyes.

There on the table was the pair of shoes, all made and finished.

The shoemaker rubbed his eyes and looked again, but it was no dream. He picked the shoes up and looked at them in wonder.

"Every stitch in place!" the shoemaker cried. "Only a master craftsman could make a shoe this fine."

That very morning, a customer tried on the shoes. The shoemaker watched him nervously, for he was afraid someone was playing a trick on him.

"These shoes are the finest I have ever seen!" said the customer, and he paid the shoemaker more than the usual price.

With this money, the shoemaker was able to buy enough leather to make two more pairs of shoes. That night, he cut the shoes out to have them ready to sew together the next morning.

But once again, he awoke to find the shoes already sewn. These were as beautiful as the first pair, and they sold quickly. With the good money paid for them, the shoemaker was able to buy leather for four pairs of shoes.

Early the next morning, the shoemaker awoke to find four pairs of shoes finished. And so it continued to happen. After a time, the shoemaker began to make a good living, and he and his wife lived quite comfortably.

One evening around Christmastime, as the shoemaker sat at his bench he looked up at his wife and said:

"If we were to stay up late tonight, we might be able to discover who has been helping us all this time."

His wife agreed. She lit a candle and the two of them hid behind some coats in the corner of the room. They waited and waited. At the stroke of midnight, two tiny elves came in and scampered over to the workbench.

Without wasting any time, they took the shoes that had been cut out and began to stitch, sew, and hammer as quick as can be. They worked so nimbly that the shoemaker and his wife were in awe. The elves did not stop until all the shoes on the workbench were finished. Then they quickly ran off again.

The next morning the wife said, "The little men have made us rich. We ought to show them how grateful we are!"

The shoemaker agreed. "But what can we do?" he asked.

"Well," said his wife, "I'm sure they must be cold, for they don't have any proper clothing. I will make them little shirts, and trousers, and warm jackets. Then I'll knit them each a pair of long woolen socks, and you can make them each a pair of shoes."

The shoemaker agreed heartily.

On the night that everything was finished, he and his wife put the gifts on the workbench, instead of the cut-out shoes. Then they both hid and waited for the elves to appear. At the stroke of midnight, the two little men came scampering through the door. But when they reached the workbench, they stopped and looked down in surprise.

All of a sudden, they burst into cackles of delight, and began trying on their new clothes. As soon as they were dressed, they began to sing:

"Now that we look so fine and dandy,
No more need to work and be handy!"

Then off they went, dancing and skipping and jumping over chairs and benches. They danced right out the door and were never seen again. But the shoemaker continued to prosper, and he and his wife lived out their days very happily.

THE FROG PRINCE

One hot summer's day a beautiful princess was sitting on the edge of a cool, deep well in the woods. In her hand was a golden ball, which she tossed in the air and caught again and again to amuse herself, until suddenly, one time, she missed it. The ball fell down into the waters of the dark well, and the princess wept as if she herself had fallen into it.

A gentle voice interrupted her weeping and asked, "What's the matter, sweet princess?"

She turned and saw that the question came from a big, ugly frog, who was sticking his thick, green head out of the water.

"My golden ball has fallen into the well," cried the princess.

"Don't worry," said the frog. "I can get it for you, but I would like something in return."

The princess offered him her gold, her jewels, even her crown, but the frog shook his head. "What I ask," he said, "is for you to love me and let me be your friend. I want to sit by you at the dinner table, eat from your plate, and sleep with you in your bed."

"Yes, of course," said the princess, not really believing that the frog could return her ball. "I'll promise you anything!"

So the frog dove down to the bottom of the well, brought the ball up in his mouth and threw it on the grass. The princess was so happy, she immediately seized the ball and forgot her promise.

"Come back!" called the frog, hopping after her. "Take me with you!" But the princess did not turn back.

That night, the princess was at dinner with her father, the king, and his royal court, when there came a strange knocking on the door, and a voice cried out, "Princess! Princess! Let me in!"

The princess ran to see who it could be and was startled to see the frog. Before she could shut the door, however, the frog hopped inside and leapt onto her chair.

The king turned to his daughter, who had gone quite pale, and asked what the frog wanted. In a halting voice, the princess told her father what had happened in the woods that day. She hoped the king would tell the ugly creature to leave.

But instead the king said, "Daughter, you must always keep your word. Now, let the frog sit with you."

The princess scowled as she set the frog in her lap, and she scowled even harder when he leaped onto the table next to her royal dinner plate.

"You promised me that I could eat from your plate," said the frog.

The king looked at her sternly and nodded his head.

Sighing, the princess pushed her plate to the frog, who ate from it so heartily that she could barely stand to look.

At last the frog finished his meal. "I'm tired now," he said to the princess. "Please take me to your room and let me lie down with you."

At that, the princess burst into tears, for she was afraid of the cold, green frog, and detested the thought of him sleeping in her clean bed. But the king had no pity for her.

"You made a promise!" said the king.

The princess angrily picked up the frog between her finger and thumb and carried him up to her room. But instead of putting him on her bed, she set him in a corner and got into bed by herself. Soon the frog hopped over to her.

"I want to sleep as much as you do," he said. "Please lift me into your bed, or I will tell your father."

This so enraged the princess that she picked him up and hurled him against the wall. "Take that, you horrid frog!" she cried.

What fell to the floor, however, was not the frog, but a prince with kind, loving eyes. He thanked the princess for delivering him from a witch's spell, and told her she was the only one who was able to release him.

The prince then requested one last promise. "Will you be my dear wife and lifelong companion?" he asked.

The princess readily agreed, and this time she was only too happy to fulfill her promise. The two were married and had a long, wonderful life together.

THE FISHERMAN
AND HIS WIFE

Long ago a fisherman sat at the edge of the sea, waiting for a fish to bite. Suddenly, his line sank down to the bottom. When he pulled it up, there was a large flounder on it. But this was no ordinary flounder.

"Please," cried the fish, "please let me go, for I'm really an enchanted prince!"

The fisherman did not need much convincing. "I would never keep any fish that talked!" he said.

So the fisherman put the flounder back in the water and watched him swim back down toward the bottom. The water was crystal clear and calm as could be. Then the man went home to his dirty hovel by the sea and told his wife what had happened.

"Didn't you wish for anything?" his wife asked.

"What for?" said the fisherman. "We're content the way we are."

"Ha!" said the wife. "How could we be happy in this horrible, dirty hovel? At least you could have asked the flounder for a pretty cottage. Go back and ask him for one. I'm sure he'll grant you anything you wish."

The man sighed and went slowly back to the sea. When he got there, the water was no longer clear and blue, but a deep green, as though a storm were brewing in the distance. The fisherman stood on the shore and said:

"Flounder, flounder, in the sea,
if you're a man, then speak to me.

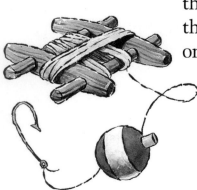

Though I do not care for my wife's request,
I've come to ask it nonetheless."

The flounder appeared and asked, "What does your wife want?"

"She thinks I should have wished for something," the fisherman said. "She thinks you're bound to give us something, since I caught you and put you back. She hates our hovel and would like to have a cottage."

"Go home then," said the flounder. "She already has it."

When the fisherman went home, his wife was sitting on a bench outside a lovely little cottage.

"Come inside!" she said, taking him by the hand. She showed him into a splendid parlor, a kitchen, and a pantry filled with fine china and good things to eat. Out back was a little yard filled with flowers and fruit trees. "Isn't this nice?" cried the fisherman's wife.

The fisherman agreed that it was very nice indeed. But if he thought his wife would be content, he was quite wrong.

After a week in their lovely cottage, the wife decided that she was tired of it. Now she wanted to live in a castle, and she begged her husband to go back to the magic flounder. With a heavy heart, he walked slowly back to the seashore and called the flounder just as he had before.

This time, the sea was dense and dark and purple, as if a storm were just on the horizon. When the fish came up, the fisherman said that his wife wanted a castle. Her wish was granted, but not long after that the fisherman returned again with another wish: his wife wanted to be king.

A few nights later, the fisherman said, "Oh wife, now you are king. Let's not wish for anything more."

But the wife disagreed. "I'm restless," she said. "Being king is fun, but I need something more. Go tell the flounder I would like to be emperor."

"But there's only one emperor in the empire!"

gasped the fisherman. "You can't be emperor, too!"

But the wife, being king, commanded her husband to make the request.

With a fearful heart, the man walked to the shore. This time, the sea was bubbling and black. A strong wind whipped across the surface and made the water curdle. Frightened, the man stepped forward and called to the flounder, who did not seem at all surprised by the wish.

When the fisherman returned home, he found a magnificent castle made of marble. Soldiers marched in front of the gate, blowing trumpets and clashing cymbals. As the fisherman walked through the doors of solid gold, he saw his wife sitting on a throne two miles high, wearing a royal gown covered in jewels. Princes, barons, and dukes stood all around her, begging for her attention.

"You're emperor now, aren't you?" the fisherman asked his wife, who answered proudly that she was. "Good," he said, "be happy with this."

"Impossible!" said the wife. "I want to be pope!"

"But you can't be!" he exclaimed.

The poor fisherman tried to explain that there was only one pope in all of Christendom, but his wife would hear none of it. They argued, but at last the husband found himself walking back to the sea. That afternoon, his wife became pope.

"At least she can't become anything greater," the fisherman thought to himself. But he was wrong.

"I would like to be God," the wife announced that evening.

"Oh, please, no!" cried the fisherman, falling to his knees.

The man's protests infuriated his wife, and she screamed at him until he set off once more.

Outside, a storm was raging so hard that the fisherman could barely stay on his feet. Houses and trees were falling, and mountains were trembling. The sky was pitch black, as were the cavernous waves that crashed upon the shore. The fisherman had to scream for the flounder to hear his call.

"What does she want this time?" asked the flounder when he rose up from the water.

"She wants to be God," cried the fisherman.

"Go back home," said the fish. "She's sitting in your hovel again."

And there, to the wife's deep regret, they are still living today.

HANSEL AND GRETEL

In a cottage at the edge of a large forest lived a woodcutter, his wife, and his two children, Hansel and Gretel. The family had fallen on hard times, and they had so little food that the wife was afraid they would soon starve.

One night, she said to her husband, "If the two of us are to live, we must get rid of the children, for we do not have enough food for them."

"Oh, no!" cried the woodcutter.

But the wife gave him no peace until he agreed.

The children, who had been kept awake by their hunger, overheard their stepmother tell their father how he was to lead the children into the woods and leave them there.

"Don't worry," whispered Hansel to his frightened sister. "I'll find a way to help us."

When his parents had gone to sleep, Hansel crept outside and filled his pockets with pebbles.

At daybreak, their stepmother shook the children awake and told them to go with their father to gather wood.

With a heavy heart, the woodcutter led his children into the forest. They walked on and on. At last, Hansel and Gretel asked if they could rest for a while.

"Of course," their father said. "I'll gather more wood, then I'll come and get you."

Instead, the woodcutter went home and left Hansel and Gretel alone in the woods, where they fell asleep. When they awoke, the woods were dark and still.

"How will we ever get home now?" cried Gretel.

"Don't worry. We'll wait until the moon comes up and lights our way," replied Hansel. "I've secretly marked our path with pebbles."

When the moon rose, the pebbles shone like silver. Hansel took his sister's hand, and the two walked until they reached home at dawn.

Their stepmother was not at all pleased to see them. "You must take them deeper into the woods next time," she whispered to her husband.

"I'd be glad to share my last crumbs with my children," the woodcutter cried sadly. But his wife gave him no peace, and he finally gave in again.

Hansel heard them, and once more he went to gather pebbles. But this time the door to the cottage was locked. "I must find a way to save us," he told himself.

The next day, Hansel and Gretel's father led them even deeper into the woods before leaving them to rest, while he returned home. Once again, Hansel and Gretel fell asleep and awoke at night. The moon shone brightly, but this time there was nothing to show them the way home.

"I marked our path with bread crumbs," Hansel told Gretel, "but the birds must have eaten them all up."

The two tried to find their way back, but they only walked deeper and deeper into the forest, growing more hungry, tired, and lost.

For two days they continued this way. On the third morning, they came to a little house in a clearing. To their delight, they found that it was made of delicious gingerbread, with a roof of whipped cream and windows of spun sugar. Hansel and Gretel wasted no time in filling their hungry stomachs with the sweet, tasty house.

Suddenly, a thin voice called out from inside,
"Nibble, nibble, like a mouse,
who is nibbling at my house?"
The children answered, "It is the wind." They went on eating, until an old woman came out of the house and invited them inside with her. There, she fed them well, and let them sleep in soft, warm beds.

But the old woman was not as kind as she seemed. She was really a wicked witch who had smelled the children from far away and had enticed them with her candy house.

The next day the witch locked Hansel in a pen and made Gretel carry rich, wonderful meals to him. "When the boy is fattened up, I will eat him!" she cackled.

Every day, the witch visited Hansel's pen, but her eyes were so bad that she could not see what the boy looked like. To help her, she made Hansel stick his finger out to feel if he was fat enough.

Knowing this, Hansel stuck out a chicken bone instead, and each day the witch found that he was still too thin. After a month, however, she lost patience and cried to poor Hansel, "I'm going to eat you anyway!"

The witch also decided to eat Gretel, whom she planned to bake in her big brass oven. That afternoon, as the witch was kneading bread, she asked Gretel to crawl inside the oven to see if it was hot enough.

Gretel, who could see flames leaping from inside the oven, guessed that the witch was trying to trick her, and pretended not to understand.

"Stupid goose!" said the witch. "This is what you do!" and she stuck her head in the oven to show her. At that, Gretel pushed the old hag all the way in and slammed the door shut.

"We're free, Hansel!" she cried, as she let him out of the pen. The two danced and sang and wandered freely about the witch's house. There, they discovered chests filled with pearls and precious

stones, and they stuffed their pockets with them before going
off to find their way home.

Hansel and Gretel walked through the woods until they came
to a beautiful lake. Just then, a large white duck appeared and
Gretel asked it to take them across on its back.

Once the children were safe on the other side, the woods grew
more familiar, until at last they saw their father's cottage.

The woodcutter was overjoyed to see his children and he swept
them up in his arms. The stepmother had died during their
absence, making their reunion a truly happy one.
With the money from the jewels Hansel and Gretel brought,
all their worries were over, and they lived happily
together for many, many years.